The Berenstain Bears

On Vacation!

Stan & Jan Berenstain

Dalmatian Press, LLC, 2010. All rights reserved. Printed in the U.S.A.
The DALMATIAN PRESS name, logo, and Tear and Share are trademarks of Dalmatian Publishing Group,
Franklin, Tennessee 37067. 1-866-418-2572. No part of this book may be reproduced or copied in any form
without written permission from the copyright owner.

10 11 12 13 NGS 36125 10 9 8 7 6 5 4 3 2
18940 Berenstain Bears Favorite Book to Color - On Vacation!

Vacation time is fun time!

It's baseball season in Bear Country.

Looks like a home run!

Hooray! The home team won!

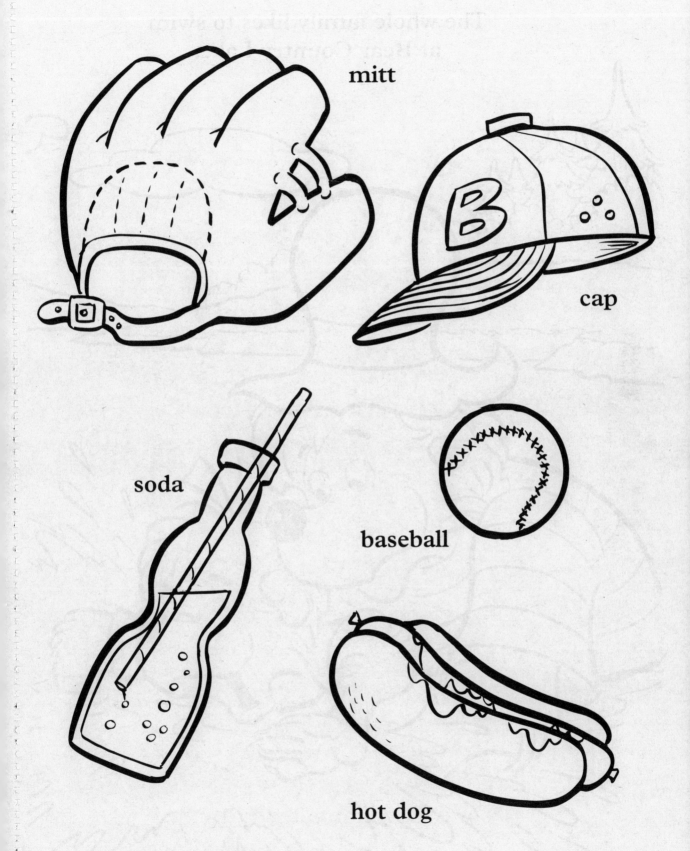

mitt

cap

soda

baseball

hot dog

The whole family likes to swim
at Bear Country Lake.

beach umbrella

beach ball

pail and shovel

sunglasses

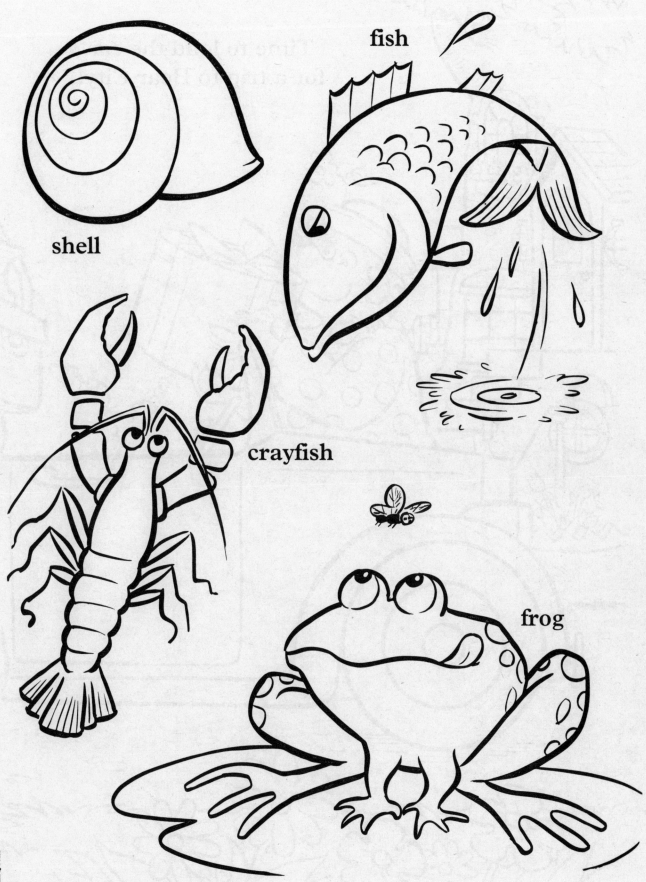

shell

fish

crayfish

frog

Time to load the car
for a trip to Bear City!

On the way they stop for
a roadside picnic.

They have lots of good food.

honey

sandwiches

cake

The fist thing they do is
go on a sightseeing tour.

BANK

BEAR

SIGHTSEEING

The cubs want to visit the Bear City Museum.

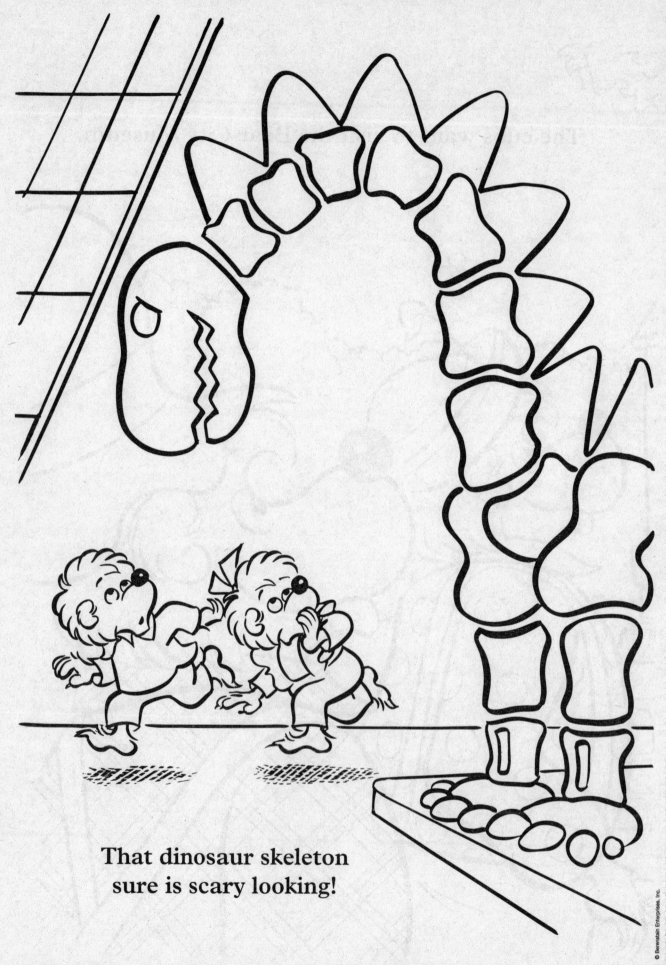

That dinosaur skeleton
sure is scary looking!

Sister and Brother like the dodo model.

Dalmatian Press

It's fun to feed
pigeons in the park.

FIRST PRESIDENT OF BEAR COUNTRY

**Great Bear Falls is the most beautiful
waterfall the Bear family has ever seen.**

The family gets a tour of
Great Bear Caverns.

On the way home they stop for pizza...

...and dessert!

banana split

ice cream soda

The vacation was wonderful,
but it is good to be home!

They will always remember
the fun they had!

I ♥ BEAR CITY

SOUVENIR OF
BEAR CITY

GREAT BEAR FALLS